THE 14TH TALE

Inua Ellams

THE 14TH TALE

OBERON BOOKS
LONDON

WWW.OBERONBOOKS.COM

The 14th Tale was first performed at Battersea Arts Centre on 31st of July 2008 performed by Inua Ellams.

Directed by Thierry Lawson
Lighting by Michael Nabarro

The play is set in a hospital waiting room and is told with flashbacks. The stage is sparse save for a chair on the far right corner. The performer wears a t-shirt and trousers splattered round the torso and pocket with red liquid giving the impression of blood.

Part 1 //

// HOSPITAL

The light that limps across the hospital floor
is as tired as I feel; it is the pale green of nausea
the shade that rises slowly, pushes upwards
and out. I want to burst, out, through, past
the sliding doors to the windy wet night, wind
my way to the kind of corners I am used to,
the kind of troubles I know and climb my way
out. But I still myself, swallow till the light
shallows, count five, four, three, two, one...

/ x /

I'm from a long line of trouble makers.
Of ash skinned Africans, born with clenched fists
and a natural thirst for battle, only quenched
by breast milk. They'd suckle as if the white silk sliding
between gums were liquid peace treaties written
from mums. Their small thumbs would dimple
the soft mounds of brown flesh, goose-pimple chests

till the ceasefire of sleep would creep into eyes,

they'd keep till the moon set and wake twice hungry,

twice vexed, raring to go. My grandfather, six years old,

tough, scatterbrained as all boys would be, once

in a gathering of tribes, crawled under tables past

the feet of tribal chiefs, surfaced by the serving dishes

cupped his hands together, began shovelling

the special treat of fried moose meat into his mouth.

When the cry of *'thief! thief!'* rang out, he turned,

wondering who had such audacity – to find an angry

line of village cooks coming his way. With his face

still stained with the spiced juice of diced moose,

he grabbed another handful and fled into the dark

woods chased by siblings, pets and abuse.

They say he ran so fast, the ground gasped, forgot

to take footprints; they lost him in the fields.

But the story never left memory, was told around

campfires and followed his son (my father)

to secondary school where a campus-wide trend

of long nicknames was maximised by a senior boy

who thumbed through a textbook's index,

added *Periplaneta Americana,* the most elaborate

he could find, to *Nevada* his old title and swaggered
through halls slapping younger boys
for mispronouncing the name.

Once, from a crowd gathered at lunch, *Periplaneta*
Americana Nevada struck six boys till father,
rebelling against seniority, revealed the title
was Latin for desert cockroach! The crowd laughed
as *Nevada* chased my father who tripped him
through a thorn bush, and the long line of trouble
makers meets me. Inheritor of fast feet and father's
contempt for authority, who, try as I might
to break the line, have battled adults, been chased
through schools and have climbed out more windows
than burglars do. I wonder which story will reach
my son and wonder more what he will do.

/ x /

It started in the hot dusty clay streets of Plateau State,
Nigeria. They say I successfully conned the doctors into
thinking I was the only one; My first trick was hiding
my twin sister for eight months and two weeks till

the shoddy equipment picked up her heartbeat:
I climbed into the world already in trouble!

By seven, I was a small, sweet-smiled pretty boy
who terrorised lizards lazing under constant suns,
had a confidence that conspired to get me caned
least once a day. But I escape one Sunday, when
the church choirs out *In the name of Jesus, in the
name of Jesus, I have a victory…* Their voices rise
like glorified sound clouds, filter through the daylight
-dyed halls to the Sunday school back-room stifled
with kids, filters to the teachers who hum along
before asking:

Oya, Oya children, did you do your homework?
Did you read the chapter that I asked you to?
Did you read your Bible? Oya, Inua, go to the front
of the class, tell us how Moses got water from the Rock.

I hadn't done the work: between *Home Alone* reruns,
tournaments of table soccer, chasing lizards, teaching
the neighbour's dog new tricks, I hadn't touched a Bible
that week, so I slouched to the front of the class
thinking wildly and chose to improvise...

Ahh teacher you know… Eh, Moses got water from the tap.

Is that so Inua?

Yes Aunty, where else?

How is that possible eh? When there weren't any pipes?

Erm… he … he had an elephant…

Searching frantic for something, anything to help,
I spied a small piece of clockwork glinting
on the classroom floor. I picked it up and inspiration,
like a white light blazed across my mind. I bit my lip
and went with it…

erm… yes, he had an elephant underground and he carved an intricate system of clockworks, of cogs and wheels and vices around the Elephant. Yes, and when he turned the tap, it turned the cogs, turned the wheels and tightened the vices around the Elephant's brokotus and he trumpeted out in pain, pushing water through his trunk, through the tap and into the ground! Yes… er… no? no?
A-ah, Aunty, Teacher! What did I do?

Stupid boy, how dare you! That is blasphemy you hear me? You are blaspheming, that is three strokes, gimme your hand jare…

> She flexed her muscles, swiping wildly with canes,
> these were long flexible raffia sticks, polished till
> they glinted as if lined with metal. Trying to put
> as much distance between me and crazed teachers,
> I dashed down the middle of the class, barrelled
> through the doorway, down the halls, out
> to the dusty courtyard with the nuns in hot pursuit,
> jumped into the tallest tree and climbed my way up
> leaving the hurricane of nuns below, praying
> and cursing me.

> They called my father. I was too high to hear voices,
> but after a minute's speak, their arms waving
> frantically, they turned, leaving Dad who asked me

down. We left the compound and walked the dusty road home in silence till he asked what happened. I told him the story. After trying not to, but finally bursting out in belly laughs, it quietened to a silence shuffled only by my feet dragging the dry road home. Nervously I asked, *Daddy, am I in trouble, will I be punished?*

No, it is too early for that to work eh, besides there is a vague order to things, things happen when they are meant to, don't worry, your time will come. Your time will come.

Part 2 //

His name was Johnny Bassey.

His name was Johnny Bassey.

Of all the troubles I have been, of those I've left
frustrated or crying, most deserving of all was he.
If ever we meet, I hope he'll have forgotten; I've
never caused anyone such pain since. In a boarding
school in Nigeria, it is a dark afternoon, mid-wet
season, all the world is grey. The torrent of rain
is a vertical river current cascading from the clouds
– all the colours dulled as though surrendered
to the storm. The trees and buildings weighted
by the water are tired, battered and drowned.
All that is alive, all that is vibrant is the chant
of *fight! fight! fight!* rising from a circle of boys,
their voices communions to gods of war, fists
pounding the air. *fight! fight!* I'm at the centre
with Jebo – my best friend – as Johnny Bassey,
the head boy eggs him on…

Jebo beat that boy! Hit him, punch him if not I'll flog you tonight! You
hear me? No Jebo Inua, beat this boy right here! fight! fight!

I try to rise above their cries, look Jebo in his eyes
and say,

Jebo don't listen to them there's no reason for us to fight for his
entertainment. Listen, if he flogs you, he'll flog me too eh?
We'll both be beaten, Jebo are you hearing me?

But Jebo is frightened, has the wild look
of a rabbit caught in lamplights, Jebo comes forward
swinging, I back away till I'm pressed against
Johnny Bassey who pushes me towards Jebo's fists,
Jebo hits me in the chest. I try to speak, try to cover
my face, fend off blows and resist retaliating,
but Jebo swings till my lips bleed, swings till I fall
to the floor, swings and comes more. Somewhere
a voice warns of a teacher coming. A circle
dissipates leaving Jebo who grabs me by my shirt and
pulls me up as I notice a dampness in his eyes…

Inua are you okay? Are you bleeding? Ah! You're bleeding! I'm really sorry, I did not mean to punch you so hard eh Inua are you okay?...

Jebo, don't touch me jor, how could you beat me eh? I am your best friend! I was talking to you!

Sorry Inua eh, but you know he beat me last week for the same thing, I couldn't let it happen again, I still have the bruises, sorry eh?

Don't touch me Jebo, go away, I don't want to see your face eh? Just go away... Jebo are you crying? Ah, it is okay, I am fine, stop crying. But we have to get him back Jebo? We have to get Johnny Bassey back.

Wait...

What are you doing tonight?

// Sound: Night. Countryside.

When the sun fell, night settled on the campus
and the only lights were pinpricks of fire flies
dancing in the still damp darkness. I called Jebo
and two close friends. Together we crept, filling
the shadows with the dark intention of ourselves,
sticking as thin as silence to the sides of the hostel

buildings, our heartbeats bursting with adrenaline,
we snaked our way to the senior's dorm.

There were four of us: one left as the look-out outside
one inside by the window I climbed through, with Jebo
– his eyes focused and keen and me with a tube
of toothpaste, *MacCleans*, bent over Johnny Bassey's
 sleeping form... Quietly, peeling back the covers,
I squeeze a thick line onto the bottom of his shirt and
press it into the fabric, squeeze a line onto each wrist,
a thick line onto the cuffs of each sleeve, thick lines
across both knuckles, lastly a line under his lower
closed eyelids, drop the finishing touches to the floor,
tickle his feet till he stirs and scarper into the dark,
stealing across the hostel grounds to the bushes.
Huddled in the fields close to the building,
we wait for it to begin.

We imagine it all: The first tingle, the cold burning
sensation, the chill that will climb up his lower eyelids,
the slow waking from dreams, the absent minded
wiping with knuckles adding to the paste, how
he'd flip his wrists, rub harder, faster, adding more,
how he'd panic, reach for cuffs, find no clean cloth,
no relief, just more pain, lift his shirt to eyes,

find no way out, roll off his bed to a floor stacked
with thumbtacks, how he'd hop!

We imagined his loud shallow cries running to the
bathroom, we laughed ourselves stupid in the bushes trying
to keep hushed. But when the scream came, so insane
was our laughter, we crashed out the bushes, collapsed
in a bundle of tears and limp limbs: a mud covered quartet
cackling into the night, laughed so loudly…

We were caught! Punished! In front of the entire
school, whipped ten strokes each and one extra
for laughing as Bassey hopped in, feet wrapped
in , patterned with polka-dots of blood,
also given a plot of elephant grassland the size
of two classes to clear with a cutlass. All things
considered, we got off lightly and as we trooped
out to the fields, still in high spirits, Jebo half-
wrestles for my cutlass saying he felt guilty,
wanted to clear my patch for me. I fought back:

Jebo, leave it alone, Jebo, it's okay eh? that's what friends are for, Jebo it's fine.

// Hospital

Can I see him now?… What do you mean *No*, I've been waiting for half an hour!… Is he okay?… Is there anything you can tell me?… THERE MUST BE SOMETHING!… Okay, I'm calm! I'm calm… Pardon?… Erm My clothes? Oh, don't worry… I'm sorry… It's just… you know… Yes a cup of water will be fine… listen, i'm really sorry about that… you know. If anything, anything at all, I'll be right here... thanks.

// Part 3

Twelve years old and I've mastered the art
of boarding school, I'm a Pro. Been punished
so much, my hands no longer blister from cutlasses
besides I've forged doctors letters declaring
I'm allergic to grass, dust and asthmatic. Pretty
useless, I'm punished to fetch endless buckets
of water but I'm working on that, I Am Working
On That! I know to sweet talk the dinner ladies
for firewood, distract them long enough for Jebo
to steal armfuls of plantains, know how to gather
stones, build campfires and roast them when
the months cold, I said it I'm a Pro. I know how
to pad my backside with text books and t-shirts
to take the pain when canes blow; I'm a Pro.

July '96, I get a phone call from home, Daddy has
a promotion, we have to leave for London, England.
Do we return? Unknown. And I cry with Jebo.
Tears hurt harder than blisters, cutlasses toothpaste,
and raffia stick, I cry all the way home, all the way
through packing, through flying, I sulk through
Heathrow Airport, through the first day of school.
Through the culture shock, through the first time

I'm called a *nig nog*… I only stop when I ask
the boy beside me:

Eh, Garri. Gaaaaryyy. Gary, where's the teacher's cane?

What?

*Gary you know? The teacher's cane? Is it made of raffia? I can handle
that one!*

What?

Gary, don't you speak English?

*Listen mate, I am bloody English and I 'eard you da first time bruv, but
teachers don't beat students bruv, dat's 'llegal, ya get me, das 'llegal!…
Wait… You mean they beat you back in Africa? Liberties! Bruv!
Liberties! Don't take that! That's deep! Liberties!*

*Shhhh Gary? Shhhh, Wait, are you saying the teachers don't have
canes? The teachers don't have canes…*

For two weeks, I go insane, I forget to walk – run
everywhere… this half-boy, half-blur, Nigerian thick-
accented black attack, scattering down halls. I jump,
glide and slide past teachers, arrive three minutes late
for each lesson, wait till the class quietens, just to burst
open doors, pause till all eyes are on me, grab
my balls and say: *ahh, just checking!*

Grandfather's feet and father's contempt for authority
catapult me across the swirling new world. I learn
new swear words, that this (masturbation) is universal,
that Mel B is the finest Spice Girl and if you spray Lynx
on a patch of fabric and breathe deeply, there's a ringing
in your ears and you giggle like little girls. Eventually,
the novelty wears, teachers see past my practised blank
stares, my African accent thins – and a new boy joins
the class, far more interesting… His name is Luis.

Dad said things happen when they are meant to,
that there's a vauge order to things… from how dust
clusters to sand particles; hardens to diamond rings,
to star alignments. From how a moose meat thief
offsprings me to how a pendulum swings; how we
read such signs shape our world and beings.

His name is Luis. He is different from me. His eyes
are thin slits with pebbles of tar for pupils, his hair
comprises of long light wisps that spill into the air
about him, his skin is the palest I've seen.
He is Chinese, doesn't speak much English, calls
his mother tongue mandarin, between you and me,
I don't like him. But mother taught me better,
so I still my tongue, smile when he tries to talk
and tag along towing this resentment.

It's the brief between humanities and maths lesson.
We know Mr Randel is off sick. Supply teachers,
all spawned from the land of useless, won't notice
four boys gone from a class of thirty so we feign
we're thirsty, ask to go back to the fountain, duck
into the boys bathroom, lift the cracked window
till it's sized enough to squeeze through and hang–
drop to the sunny outside by the bike sheds. There
is Jack, Daniel, Luis and Me. The ground is a mosaic
of decayed leaves, splashed bird droppings and
cigarette butts. None of us smoke: we spend the first
few minutes getting over the fear of being caught,
then we begin to talk.

Now, we don't speak of video games, cars, girls or films
- the usual topics the minds of boys skim, instead
with voices high, pitched in excited tones, we speak
of excrement. Shit. In such detail do our tongues roam.
We speak of the floaters, the sleepers, small pellets
that seem ricochet out, the mammoth ones, and tough
number twos that seem to fight back! Jack mimes
facial expression, pushes and strains till his skin stains
red, Daniel makes the sound effects, I *phew* and *whew*
the redder Jack gets and Luis who vaguely understands
begins to laugh. And perhaps all this talk summons
the forces of nature for five minutes later, it gets real.

We line up against the school walls
with an uncontrollable urge and begin to pee.
Luis catches on and joins as our hips snake and
spell our names…

I.N.U.A. Luis… Luis… wait for the fullstop.

Plop!

Now, whenever I pee, just before the custom to stretch,
shake and ensure there are no drops are left, I get this

funny sensation you know. It begins as a tickle, a soft
stroke between my shoulder blades, slows down my
spine, gathers momentum and explodes in a ticklish
uncontrolled spasm. I've known this for as long as
I've known time. Of the four boys who passed urine,
only one spasmed as I and turning, found surprising to
my eyes, Luis to share this shudder,
my spine. And here is where the vague order to things
come, where how we read such signs change our world
and beings… this is no star alignment, no pendulum
swing, but finding Luis to share this shudder, my spine
sparked a new way of thinking.

Since then, I've looked on all strange men as possible
brothers in spine. That regardless of race age, colour or
creed, brotherhood is an undiscovered shudder away.
So excited am I, my accent blacks back to African,
I babble incoherently to

Luis, don't you get it, my spine tingles, Your spine tingles, tingling
spine…

Through the thick of Mandarin he gets it. He gets it
and draped over each other, we laugh as if we sniffed
a can of Lynx each. Jack and Daniel don't get it. I try

to explain through stomach cramps and Luis arms,
when a passing girl hears the havoc our voices, turns
the corner sees us and runs to get a teacher. We grab
bags and jackets, get ready to run… then realise our
names are wet, dripping, written on the school walls.
Caught, we're punished for skipping class and defiling
school property. As for the girl, I get her back!

Night fall finds me home. Through mouthfuls
of jollof rice, I tell Dad about Luis's spine
and vengeance. Dad laughs, reminds:

Listen oh, you must grow out of this someday.

Then adds,

Okay, your time will come, just don't get caught.

The plan is simple. Her name is Stacey Flood.
She is as wide as she is tall. Wears too tight Levis
501s that funnel past her waist when she sits.
If you're unfortunate to catch a glimpse, you'll see
a flat mashed freckle-speckled-chicken-raw ass
the size of the grand canyon staring back.

I wait patient as a rock face till she snoozes
in the dinner hall like she usually does, creep
towards her flanked by Jack and Luis...

Shhhhs! Get back! You'll wake her! Shhhushs

Slowly I take out a package wrapped in kitchen foil
that I sweet talked the dinner ladies into leaving
in the freezer, ease back the silver sheet, prise apart
two ice-cubes: between sits a cold frozen 5p coin.
I dangle it over Stacy's soft cheeks, line it with
the cavern of her grand canyon, where her butt
splits...and let it go...

Ahhhhh!!!!

Luis did you see that? Jack we got her back! That was priceless!

// Hospital

I can see him now?... Thanks, thank you so much...
Okay Inua, breathe, four, three, two, one... Hello,
hey... I'm good thanks. You?... Pardon? No, this...
don't worry about it... So what are the doctors
saying?... A what?... In your BRAIN!?... You

may never… No?… It's too soon…What? What do you mean visiting hours are over? Okay, five more minutes… They have to runs tests. They couldn't possibly know that yet… Mm hmmm… yes but… Pardon? Just two more minutes! Just… damn! Okay… Okay. I'll see you tomorrow… first thing… Okay?… Bye… bye.

They say he may never walk again.

Ireland

Part 4

Mid-teens we moved to Dublin, to a world more
alien than London was, a world so far from Nigeria,
I was the only Black boy in school. First break time,
the attempt to blend in didn't work. Feeling like
a weed in the gnarled garden of Ireland's green,
a reluctant ambassador for Africa, I spruced up
my image, tried to stay clean, but still trouble came…

There was the parent's evening when, commenting
on mothers walking past, I spotted a thin-waisted
red-headed Celtic dazzler drifting across the car park,
nudged the boys, said…

Oi, would yous look at that ride!

The guys on the left collapsed in hysterics whilst
a deathly silence owned the right, I turned
to catch Ross Lynch, star rugby player, an inch
from my face say

Ross hunted me for three days straight, stalked me
through the emerald/grey maze of school. I evaded
capture with Grandfathers's feet, but was too slow
for that Friday by the gates when, after waving
goodbye to friends, I didn't hear the

WATCH OUT!

till it was too late, everyone scattered, Ross rode
into me on his moped, engine snarling, spitting
fire, front wheel cannoned into my chest, back-
wheel spun over my pelvis, I staggered home
with skid marks on my crotch!

There was the Saturday night we invaded school,
fashioned hoops from dustbins, played basketball
on the rooftop. I learnt the hard way – life doesn't flash
past when death threatens. Four points into the game,
police sirens sliced the night. We scrambled low
over the rooftops, tried to hang-drop off the three-
storey building when the brick I tightly gripped came

loose. Slipping into the black nothingness, the fatality
of a fall screamed through me till Ross (now the good
friend) grabbed my hands and hauled me up.
I trembled as we ran across the green, dodging
police torch lights like laser beams.

I left the green of Ireland singed with a Celtic fire
and a mishmashed accent of the straight speak
of Africans, stiff lip cockney and the thrust
of Southern Dublin, arrived in London more
scatterbrained than ever!

/ x /

Time passed tumultuous, trouble flared, but in feline
form where even the weather, famed for disrupting
the transport system; the inch of rain which would
stay workers away, even a freak winter cold or the now
often blizzards, or night-reports that warned *Stay
indoors, don't stray from home,* even that couldn't
hold me back from six months with Ella, whose chin
was porcelain-perfect with four freckles like dust
speckles I'd tickle till she laughed, or five months

with Anna, finest nose from Southern France, au pair,
from Brockwell who danced to deep trance, or four
months with Paris, ex Parisian/Persian queen! Whose
skin glowed golden and tinged a touch olive, or nine
months with Boden, feisty hockey player, always
bruised from head to toe, save the small of her back
which would flutter if you touched it like loose tissues
stacked against breeze; even gale force never held
me back, scatterbrained, I'd hack across city, cross
town until one stopped me frozen, dead in my tracks.

Her name was Donna Lorde and she had lashes
that lazed the world. Hair that cascaded crazily, locks
that kept me captive. I did not seek freedom, wanted
to stay captivated by long looks and her flowing mane
of wild stallions, formed of powder puffs and pouts,
she was gorgeous. We met on a night ordained by
the ordinary. The stars reflected in the window pane
dribbled mere suggestions of light that mingled with
the rain. I told her that I would like to see her again
and lip-printed her left cheek. A week later, sheltered
from London's lazy rain, we first-kissed, our tongues
like dancers, lips the dance-floor, heart beating
the backing track to tongue tip tango, kissing as though
Shango flung small sweetened lightening bolts

between us like firework-flavoured mangoes…
In this fruit frenzy and lightening shift, she tells me
she does not do relationships. That should have sent
alarm bells ringing but I was caught between wild
stallions and electric mangoes. All I remembered
was a comma in a cascading kiss… besides, no-strings
-attached loving was a luxury I could not miss, so I'm
like:

Yeah, that's what I'm talking about!

Three weeks later, I know her mind to be greater
than her fine body's form, I want to be the duvet
that keeps her warm, to be there when brain waves
collide so I can ride its after surf till the morning
comes. She senses this change, in me, reminds me
she does not do relationships, I reply

Yeah, I know

But harbouring fugitive fantasies of us with entwined
shadows, I did not want to let go: It started with me
holding on long after we'd stop kissing, with waking

up at night to watch her chest rising, and falling and
perspiring forehead glisten, with whispering her first
name with my surname just making sure it fits.

She, sensing this changing growing started un-sowing
those lightning seeds till our bouts became sparse
forays where my heart showing caused her to freeze.
I tried giving her space to breathe, that a graceful
absence might make her see that though laced
with thoughts of lengthening light seeds, this could still
be easy… Till she tells me this has gone too far, has
pushed past friendship to something greater. That type
of feast she just cannot cater. She stays away for a week.

/ x /

I go round unannounced with a bouquet of rose
flowers: my hopes and dreams soft and tainted as
the fragrance in my arms, reach to push the doorbell
and hear laughter waft from the second floor window,
step back, peek, I see another man, head thrown back,
her face delicately pressed to his, her hair cascades
softly, she whispers to him, voice tickling his throat…

And all I see is black, all I taste is venom, all I feel
is anger, the dark fired kind, such rage, such rage,
I shred the roses to pieces, thorns tear into my hands,
palms bleed. I pace in the opposite side of the street,
think black, think venom, think fire, think and plot,
think and plot till he leaves. Then inspired by blood
and roses disappear for an hour, return under the cover
of dusk with pockets filled.

I cross over to stand in the shadows of the tree
that punches through the pavement, grows up
beside her open bathroom window. It is night
and there's venom in my eyes. I climb up, inch
my way through the rough foliage of trees, leaves
rustle like a thousand nuns' voices asking me down
I crush their stems like throats, climb up till I'm lined
with the bathroom window, stretch, grab, pull
and arch myself over, through and land softly
on the bath mat.

It is so quiet, the moonlight bouncing round the room
makes noise. It licks the tiled walls, tooth brushes,
towels and the shower curtain I draw back, reach,
pluck the shower head from its hold, gently unscrew
the metal cap. Taking from my pocket two jumbo-sized

tubes of red acrylic paint, I squeeze till the tubes
are flat and emptied into the shower head and try
to screw the metal cap back on. With each twist
it squeaks but in the death silence of the night
it sounds like tombstone dragged against stone,
I slow down, twist, twist twist…

// Sound of phone ringing.

*Hello? Hi… Hi… listen Sis, this is not a good time. I
can't talk right now…Erm Hi Donna! Calm down, stop
screaming! It is Inua, It's just me… Sis, I'm kinda busy, just
in the middle of something… Donna, don't call the police!
You'll wake the neighbours, It's not a good idea!…
Listen Sis, I'm in the middle of something, just
call me back… Hello?… What?… Donna shhhshs!…
Hospital? I'm coming… Donna sorry, I have to go…*

Part 5 //

// Hospital

Time freezes in the hospital ward.
The doctor's words gather about me and tower
till a shadow – dark as uncertainty – falls tangling
everything. Rooted in the hospital ward,
for the first time, ever, I am frozen, I am still.
This is beyond trouble. There is no authority
to contempt, no walls, no teachers… no…

My father had a stroke. A blood vessel burst
bleeding into the right side of his brain, cutting
signals to the left side of his body. The muscles
there are stiff, only half his face moves, his speech
is slurred, he cannot walk. He rolls off his bed
when he sleeps so has to be strapped in with
a tangle of white tubes and wires. A nightmare
of machines and monitors bleep, flash in random
patterns – a mayhem of lights and life flickering.

Boys should never see their fathers fall.
It upturns worlds and steals words. No longer
thorn of authority, living legacy of troublemakers,
overnight, Dad becomes just a man. And I his son,
mortal – unable to run.

Weeks pass in the hospital ward. I watch Dad drift
in and out of consciousness till one Friday the sun
spills a half-light that ghosts over hunched shoulders
into my cupped palms. I hold a Bible and read Dad
psalms, but my tears blur the letters. I read in
stuttered staccato that wakes Dad from sleep.
Drowsily he peeks from the folds of hospital clothes,
catches me and the Bible both dripping tears.
In short slurred words, he asks why I cry
and I want to tell him why. How it is too soon
for him to go. How suddenly I feel disconnected
from the line, alone as a barefooted child walking
a dusty road home in silence, asking the world
Why? Instead I say

I don't know.

And he laughs. Because he's seen it all before, says

There is a vague order to things… things happen for a reason. Don't worry, I'll be fine. Maybe… time has come eh?

and I accept this. I let it wash over, let it come…
And slowly, things begin to unravel; a vague order
begins to rise. Uncles and aunts call with demands
and questions… My instant contempt for authority
falls as I note the motives, the fear in their words.
Dad comes home, I master how to tiptoe. Evenings,
go for walks, speed has to be controlled. I slow down
as Dad learns to walk again. Broken brain wires spark
and form again. We talk of the past, tempt the future,
litter it with song, tickle it with laughter…

They say when death laughs at a man, all a man
can do is laugh back. We work by lamplight.
Dad writes a letter. I research how stroke victims
are prone to second ones, when the lamp dies.
He reaches out into the death-defined darkness,
unscrews the light bulb, delicate in his back-to
-nimble left hand, and laughs.

In the darkness, my chest swells like a sunrise,
such light, it bleaches the living room, breaches
the dusk, reaches back and stops time for the souls
of trouble makers who form a vague line, Dad
beckoning that I take my place in front of these
Ash-skinned-Africans, born with clenched fists
and a natural thirst for battle, only quenched
by breast milk.

I've battled adults, been chased through schools, have
climbed out more windows than burglars do. Finally,
through the vague order of these things, my time has
come like Dad said it would. I wonder when this story
will reach my son and wonder more what he will do.

END.